The hairy fairy

"I wish I had a bigger bike," said Rob to his mum. "Tim and Kim both have much bigger bikes. If only I had a bigger bike I'd be happy."

2

"Be happy with what you have, my boy," said Mum, "or you might get a visit from the hairy fairy."
"What hairy fairy?" asked Rob.

"Haven't I ever told you about the little old woman and the hairy fairy?" said his mum.
"Well, it was like this ..."

Once upon a time there was
a little old woman who lived
in a small, broken down, wooden hut.
One day the hairy fairy was passing the
door when she found the little old
woman talking to herself.

4

"Oh dear, it's a shame. Oh dear, it's a shame," said the little old woman.
"I didn't ought to live in a small, broken down, wooden hut. If only I had a little cottage, with roses around the door, I'd be happy, that I'd be!"

5

So the hairy fairy waved her hairy fairy
wand and said,
"Very well, before you go to bed tonight,
turn around three times, scratch your
head, kiss the cat, and in the morning
you'll see what you will see."

Before she went to bed, the little old
woman turned around three times,
scratched her head, kissed the cat ...

and in the morning to her delight
she found that she was in a little
cottage, with roses around the door.

But, the little old woman quite forgot
to thank the hairy fairy.

The hairy fairy flew north and she flew south, she flew east and she flew west, and one day she thought that she'd go to see the little old woman in her little cottage, with roses around the door.

8

"Oh dear, it's a shame. Oh dear, it's a shame," said the little old woman.
"I didn't ought to live in a little cottage, with roses around the door. If only I had a little house, with lace curtains and a brass knocker on the door, I'd be happy, that I'd be!"

So the hairy fairy waved her hairy fairy
wand and said,
"Very well, before you go to bed tonight,
turn around three times, scratch your
head, kiss the cat, and in the morning
you'll see what you will see."

Before she went to bed, the little old
woman turned around three times,
scratched her head, kissed the cat ...

and in the morning to her delight
she found that she was in a little house,
with lace curtains and a brass knocker
on the door.

But, the little old woman quite forgot
to thank the hairy fairy.

The hairy fairy flew north and she flew south, she flew east and she flew west, and one day she thought that she'd go to see the little old woman in her little house, with lace curtains and a brass knocker on the door.

"Oh dear, it's a shame. Oh dear, it's a shame," said the little old woman. "I didn't ought to live in a little house, with lace curtains and a brass knocker on the door. If only I had a big house, with a long drive and a smart new car, I'd be happy, that I'd be!"

So the hairy fairy waved her hairy fairy wand and said,
"Very well, before you go to bed tonight, turn around three times, scratch your head, kiss the cat, and in the morning you'll see what you will see."

Before she went to bed, the little old woman turned around three times, scratched her head, kissed the cat ...

and in the morning to her delight
she found that she was in a big house,
with a long drive and a smart new car.

But, the little old woman quite forgot
to thank the hairy fairy.

The hairy fairy flew north and she flew south, she flew east and she flew west, and one day she thought that she'd go to see the little old woman in her big house, with a long drive and a smart new car.

"Oh dear, it's a shame. Oh dear, it's a shame," said the little old woman.
"I didn't ought to live in a big house, with a long drive and a smart new car. If only I had a castle, with lots of servants to pamper me, I'd be happy, that I'd be!"

So the hairy fairy waved her hairy fairy
wand and said,
"Very well, before you go to bed tonight,
turn around three times, scratch your
head, kiss the cat, and in the morning
you'll see what you will see."

Before she went to bed, the little old
woman turned around three times,
scratched her head, kissed the cat ...

and in the morning to her delight
she found that she was in a castle, with
lots of servants to pamper her.

But, the little old woman quite forgot
to thank the hairy fairy.

The hairy fairy flew north and she flew south, she flew east and she flew west, and one day she thought that she'd go to see the little old woman in her castle, with lots of servants to pamper her.

"Oh dear, it's a shame. Oh dear, it's a shame," said the little old woman.
"I didn't ought to live in a castle, with lots of servants to pamper me. If only I was the queen herself, in a huge white palace, and had a throne and jewels, and everyone waving at me!
Then I really would be happy!"

So the hairy fairy waved her hairy fairy wand and said,
"Very well, before you go to bed tonight, turn around three times, scratch your head, kiss the cat, and in the morning you'll see what you will see."

Before she went to bed, the little old woman turned around three times, scratched her head, kissed the cat, and in the morning ...

to her horror she found that she was
back in her small, broken down, wooden
hut.

The hairy fairy flew north and she flew south, she flew east and she flew west, but she never came back to the old woman again – never ever!

OK Mum, my bike's fine!